Janey Crane

Barbara deRubertis
Illustrated by Eva Vagreti Cockrille

The Kane Press
New York

Cover Design: Sheryl Kagen

Library of Congress Cataloging-in-Publication Data

DeRubertis, Barbara.
Janey Crane/Barbara deRubertis; illustrated by Eva Vagreti Cockrille.
p. cm.
"A Let's read together book."

Summary: Janey plans to surprise her friends by baking their favorite cakes to
celebrate her birthday, but she is the one who gets surprised.
ISBN 1-57565-022-3 (pbk. : alk. paper)
[1. Birds--Fiction. 2. Birthdays--Fiction. 3. Cake--Fiction. 4. Stories in rhyme.]
I. Vagreti Cockrille, Eva, ill. II. Title.
PZ8.3.D455Jan 1997   96-52643
[E]--dc21   CIP
                                                        AC

10 9 8 7 6 5 4

First published in the United States of America in 1997 by The Kane Press.
Printed in China.

LET'S READ TOGETHER is a registered trademark of The Kane Press.

Janey Crane
is now awake.
She gives her tail
a little shake.

She shakes her legs.

She shakes her wings.

She shakes her head.

And then she sings.

5

"My friends don't know
today's the day!
My birthday is
today! Hoo-ray!

6

"To celebrate,
I'll bake a cake.
A tasty cake
is what I'll make.

"I'll have a party
at the lake.
Then all my friends
can share my cake!"

Janey calls to
Jake the Drake.
"Meet me later
at the lake!

"Tell Daisy Quail and Ray the Jay. I'll have a big surprise today!

"Jake the Drake
likes carrot cake.
A carrot cake
is what I'll make."

Janey starts
to scrape and grate.
The carrot cake
will taste just great.

"But Daisy Quail
likes raisin cake.
I'll make TWO cakes,
for goodness sake."

Janey starts
to shake and quake.
A raisin cake
is fun to make.

"And Ray the Jay
likes acorn cake.
Okay. Today,
THREE cakes I'll make!

"The acorn shells
are hard to break.
But acorn cake
is what I'll make."

The cakes are baking.
Janey waits.
And while she waits,
she gets three plates.

Hooray! The carrot
cake is great!
She places it
upon a plate.

The raisin cake
is light as air.
She tips it on
the plate with care.

The acorn cake
is heavy weight!
She takes it to
the biggest plate.

Janey makes
a big "A" frame.
She stacks the cakes.
It's like a game!

Then Janey places
all the cakes
upon her head.
A big mistake!

She's late. She runs.
She's on her way.
Take care! Beware!
LOOK OUT FOR RAY!

Ray the Jay says,
"What a shame!"
Janey wails,
"I am to blame!

"I really did not
use my brain.
Oh, what a mess!"
cries Janey Crane.

Ray says, "Janey,
it's okay!
The ants will eat
your cakes today!

"Just hear them rave
about the taste!
You see? Your cakes
won't go to waste."

Then Janey wails,
"There's more to do.
I must tell Jake.
And Daisy, too."

Ray says, "Janey,
come this way.
We know your birthday
is today!"

32